THE CONNECTOR

Comparing scenes

from dreams

to actual life experiences.

Renee Alter

Contents

Introduction

Everything is connected. When I became aware of this, the Universe began to appear filled with dots that connected with my thoughts and life experiences. I began meeting people who reflected intentions that I made, such as a teacher of a subject I decided I wanted to know more about. My life began to shift with increasing scenarios as described by Law of Attraction. Set an intention, imagine the situation already exists, expect it to happen, and suddenly it could appear.

I began to call myself "The Connector" after seeing a pattern that many of the people I randomly met were just the people I was looking for. People I thought about visiting or calling would just happen to be in the same store I went to at the same time I went. Many times I'd find out that people I randomly met in completely different places knew each other or would eventually be connected to each other through me. Thus, I thought of myself as a dot. And if I was a dot, so was everyone else, and we were all supposed to be connected.

Jenny is a fictitious character who weaves in and out of time and space through her dreams and other realities – connecting the dots between them. The dreams are from my actual 'dream' journal, and the rest is based on real life experiences when I realized the connections between the dreams and my 'reality.' The final chapter is fantasy with a splash of reality. The term reality is used loosely as from what I've learned, reality is relative to an individual's perception.

Dream: World War II Scene

Jenny stood up from the large steel desk and straightened the skirt of her grey uniform. She gathered the paperwork she had been working on and placed the stack neatly into a folder. She placed the folder into a drawer and locked it with the small key on her key ring. The clock on the wall displayed 5:01 PM, and the German military officer who had been working in another room emerged, asking her if she was ready to go.

Outside, a driver in uniform waited by the 1941 black Chevrolet sedan. The driver opened the back door so Jenny and the officer could climb inside. Darkness was fast approaching as the sun set over the horizon. Jenny looked forward to getting home to her four-year-old blond-haired, blue-eyed son, left in the care of a baby-sitter. The boy's father had been killed in the war.

During the twenty minute drive, the officer engaged Jenny in conversation about the boy, sharing that he had a grandson that age. As they approached the apartment building where Jenny lived, the conversation was interrupted by a flash of light and a loud explosion. The driver was instructed to pull over. A cloud of dust filled the air, and as the breeze began to blow it aside, Jenny panicked. A corner of the apartment building she lived in had blown off.

The driver hopped out of the car and opened the back door to let both of them out. Jenny began to run while time seemed to be suspended. She ran into the building and began to run up the stairs to the third floor where she lived. When she got to her door, she discovered it was ajar, and there were no occupants in the unit. Where was her son?

Jenny turned and ran back down the stairs and smacked into the officer who was standing at the entrance to the building. She began to scream: "My son!

My son! Where is he?" Adrenaline pumped through her body as she felt consumed with fear. Then she woke up.

Reality: Comparison to the Dream

As Jenny's pulse was still racing, she pulled opened the journal she kept by her bed and wrote what she could remember of the dream. It seemed so REAL. How could a dream feel so real? Most of her dreams had random weird scenes like the ones when she was trying to run away from something chasing her and could only crawl. Eventually, this dream became one where she was able to lift off the earth and weightlessly jump across rooftops. There were all the strange dreams of her driving different vehicles in which the brakes wouldn't work, but she woke up each time before she crashed.

The boy in the dream had looked very much like her real son had looked when he was four. He was now approaching 21 years of age. Had she lived other lives? Was this one of them? The dream seemed to take place during World War II, and when she looked through images of the types of cars that were being driven during that time, she found the Chevy she had seen in the dream. In the dream, she was a single mother, just like she was in her current life. In the dream, she was a secretary just like she was in her current life. She recalled the time when her son had walked off when he was three, and she couldn't find him. Twenty minutes felt like an eternity as she ran all over the apartment complex looking for him. With increased panic, she ran out toward the main boulevard and saw the old man holding her son's hand as they were walking toward the apartments. Her son had decided to go to the bus stop on his own and get on the bus. The old man had intercepted him.

World War II had involved Germany and Japan. In the dream, Jenny lived in Germany. Now many of the women she had been meeting were from Germany, and her son had married a Japanese girl. It was odd that she had not met any German men. The German women had married American military and moved to the United States with them. Were these circumstances coincidence? And what had happened to the boy's father in the dream? The actual father of her son in this life was thirteen years older than she was and had been in the military, too. He didn't want the responsibility of another child, so Jenny had left when she was three months pregnant. Another coincidence?

Dream: Library Scene

Jenny sat at a large round table in the Central Texas College library with a loose-leaf notebook open on the table. The desk was in front of a large window which looked out into a beautiful garden. After staring out at the garden for about five minutes, she brought her attention back to her writing project. She began by studying the mind map she drew on a blank piece of paper of the various scenes she planned to build around a central plot. She closed her eyes with the intent of letting some words flow through, trusting she would receive them from the grand master of all thoughts.

A few minutes later, Jenny opened her eyes and looked up at the reflection in the window of the tall man with dark hair, a mustache, and a beard standing behind her. He was wearing a black yarmulke, so she assumed he was Jewish. She saw him looking over her right shoulder at what she was writing, so Jenny turned around and said hello.

The man asked permission to sit down across from her and began to talk about what she was writing. He said he was a psychologist and a Rabbi and was working on a book himself. They conversed for about thirty minutes when he excused himself to go to another appointment and left. Then Jenny woke up.

Reality: The Rabbi

How very odd that Jenny saw this man in the dream, and at a college where she wasn't enrolled. The dream was realistic and unlike so many other dreams that did not make any sense. Was it a prophetic one?

Months after having this dream, Jenny saw a white van with a Star of David on the side of it entering her local post office parking lot as she was leaving. Since she was Jewish and had not met any other Jewish people in the town she had moved to, she stopped to ask the man if he was, too. He told her he was a Rabbi and that to support his family, he was delivering pharmaceutical supplies on a 200-mile route.

Just five minutes away from where Jenny was living, a female minister had a thrift store where she had been going regularly. It was a small world when the

Rabbi told her that he had been stopping in there as well. He was also planning to speak for one of her upcoming events, so Jenny was invited to attend. Jenny went to the event and met the Rabbi's wife and children which gave her a sense of trust to accept his generosity.

Jenny had told the Rabbi that she was living alone in an old motor home out in a field in the middle of nowhere and had been suffering from health challenges that included depression. For the next six months, he stopped by where she lived once a week to check on her and many times gave her some money. On one of her worst days, he told her she could go stay with him and his family – an hour away, but she declined. Had the dream she had been a prophetic one?

Dream: The Collapsing Stairway

Jenny stood on the stairway of the third floor of the house in Massachusetts she grew up in. But something was different. It had a railing on an 'open' part – and the two rods on the end were loose, so she took them off. Then like a domino effect, the entire railing all the way down began to collapse.

A heavy-set black woman appeared at the top of the stairs wearing a royal blue stretchy evening gown... one side of the dress along the leg was tapered up to her waist. Jenny knew the lady, but from where?

In a completely different scene of the same dream, Jenny had boarded an old bus with her son who was still very little. The bus driver was the same black woman who had appeared at the top of the stairs. They had taken the bus to the end of the route, but it wasn't home. Jenny had asked where she could get the bus to "home" and was directed to another terminal. She had to walk a long way, pushing her son in an umbrella stroller, crossing over a major throughway.

Suddenly Jenny was back at the stairwell. The black woman looked at the collapsing railing and picked up an armful of railing pieces – but more pieces kept appearing – so she left. Then Jenny woke up.

Reality: The Psychic

Months later, Jenny met a woman at a laundromat who looked just like the lady in the dream; however, the scenes in the dream took place at two different time zones, which was very confusing. Jenny didn't understand the significance of the collapsing railing… unless it represented the upcoming collapsing of her life.

The woman Jenny met turned out to be a psychic – working part-time at the laundromat temporarily for extra income. After exchanging just a few words, the lady came up very close to Jenny and told her that she was asleep, and it was time to wake up!

Jenny's world began to swirl. Which was the real world? The ones in the dreams or the ones she thought she was in now? Why was this woman telling her it was time to wake up? Jenny asked for her phone number because the lady wouldn't tell her anything else while she was working.

A few days later, Jenny arrived at the lady's house. She was told that she was overmedicated, and Jenny couldn't remember hardly anything else that was said. She just went home and decided to stop taking the eleven prescription medications she had been taking every day cold turkey. She endured five days of withdrawal followed by waking up!

In the midst of the wake-up, she was downloaded by a heavenly source with life instructions that included writing, and she began to write all kinds of stories most of the days and most of the nights. Insomnia and adrenaline rushes kept her awake as information came pouring through her fingers onto paper.

Adrenaline coursing through her body also cancelled out sensations of pain. This lasted several months before the metaphorical staircase she saw in the dream began to collapse. It was her life. Suddenly the dream made sense. Everything Jenny knew had to collapse to make room for something new to develop.

While the several months after the drug withdrawal was filled with creative energetic days, it was temporary. Another stage of development was in store. Jenny crashed like the collapsing railing into PTSD, depression, anxiety attacks, and pain made worse by chronic insomnia. She didn't want to just start taking all the medications again, so she avoided her doctor and began to research everything she could find on her own about alternative solutions.

Eventually, Jenny found many of the answers she had been seeking, and she began the process of building a new flight of stairs. She finished writing six books and a half dozen new songs followed by meeting other authors and musicians. She taught herself social media and built a website with a blog. She learned more about Natural Medicine and made different food choices. She even joined Curves and began a regular exercise regime. Plus, she indulged her imagination with unlimited possibilities for her future.

Dream: Theme Park

Jenny was enthralled at the theme park she found herself in. People were climbing into pods shaped like walnuts in their shells that were being catapulted out across the shoreline and into the middle of the water. Would she be brave enough to try it?

Cars were lined up go get on a ferry which brought them to the machine that was called the "Catapult." How could so many pods be thrown without crashing into each other? She stood alone by the fence watching people climb into pods, which flew through the air, and landed in the water. She watched the pods open and float in the water with their occupants as they acclimated to air again. Then she woke up. Or maybe she didn't.

Suddenly, Jenny was on a Disneyland-type ride in a cart that was going through a long, dark tunnel. ETs with white, unclothed bodies and large dark eyes appeared in her cart and gently began massaging the knotted muscles in her body. Time stood still as she relaxed into the experience. Their fingertips were warm and soft as they did not have fingernails. This dream had felt very realistic, too. But alas, she woke up.

Reality: Interconnectedness

Videos of extraterrestrials using walnut-shaped pods to travel in began to appear on Jenny's Facebook feed posted by a site called In5D. In one of them, messages of hope from beings from other planets spoke of coming to the earth if they are asked from the heart. According to the 'report,' ETs had already been on earth to neutralize nuclear weapons and atom bombs as the blasts would rock their worlds as well as ours. She read articles about the near future collapse of the dollar which would result in all debts being erased. More articles appeared about government corruption. Everything collapsing.

The lady at the laundromat had been distraught by the visions in her own prophetic dreams, feeling the pain of the earth being destroyed as well as all the life that was on it. The lady in the previous dream had tried to pick up all the pieces, but couldn't. Jenny was connecting the dots and wishfully erased the disturbing visions.

Jenny began to listen to more videos – this time by Gregg Braden – who talked about the interconnectedness of all of existence. He said that the ancient biblical texts that were left out of our bible explained how our emotions affect our health and the world around us – that prayers were not meant to be said in words but with feelings. He had gone to Tibet and other ancient places where he learned the truth of our beginnings. He asked the monks what it is they do in their prayers and was told they do whatever it took to have the emotions necessary to create the result they expected. He explained that when we connect our thoughts with our heart, believing that the outcome of what we want has already happened, only then can our prayers be answered. And finally, that it wouldn't take that many people to influence the outcome of world events by holding the Universe in our hearts and believing in peace.

Jenny chose to believe that there was enough love to save everything worth saving. She chose to focus on thoughts of love and people living together peacefully. She chose to focus on having enough of everything for herself and the rest of the planet. Each night before falling asleep, she visualized energy from her heart expanding outward into all of life.

Fantasy:

Healing by an Extraterrestrial

Then there came a day an extraterrestrial decided it was time to visit Jenny. The ET was standing by Jenny's bed when she woke up that morning, and touched her tenderly where her heart was, adding to its expansion of energy with love. She felt healing warmth spread throughout her body, and the aches she usually woke up with melted away.

The ET then touched Jenny's forehead (her third eye) and she began to see rainbows of colors followed by visions of what she presumed to be a joyous future for Earth filled with cooperative communities and beautiful gardens. The ET invited Jenny to stand up and follow it into a cyclical pod that appeared in the middle of her bedroom. She followed the ET into the pod, and suddenly they appeared in what looked like their spaceship.

After being led to a room that appeared to be an exam room, the ET communicated to Jenny telepathically, and she was guided to take off her clothes, change into a lavender exam gown, and lay down on one of the warm soft exam tables. She felt confident that they meant no harm to her and followed their instructions.

As the beings did not wear clothes and did not appear to have any sex organs, Jenny could not tell if they were male or female. The one closest to her passed a fluoroscope over her body, and a screen on the ceiling as well as on a table showed all the systems of her body – much more advanced than the ones used on Earth. When the scan was complete, a report printed out. The being showed Jenny some dark spots signifying energy holes and asked if she'd like them to be repaired. Of course!

Next, the being used a sound device to "fill up the holes," strengthening Jenny's porous vertebrae, and fixing the anomaly in her lower back. She was shown before and after x-rays. Yes, finally! She had been holding the belief that a new technology would fix her porous vertebrae and align her spine but never imagined that it would not be done on Earth!

Jenny was then led to a warm pool of rainbow colored water to step into after removing the gown. Since the ETs weren't wearing cloths, she did not feel self-conscious about being naked. The water was filled with tiny rainbow-colored bubbles, and she felt all her chakras glow brighter from inside of her. While in the water, she also became aware of the inner neural networks throughout her body – just like she had seen them on videos of babies developing in their mothers' wombs. Then she laid back for a floating meditation.

While floating in the water, Jenny thought about being touched in a way that would heal all her past emotional wounds and traumas. ETs materialized before her inner eyes and began touching her in therapeutic ways, easing the stress out of every tight muscle. They were hearing her requests telepathically and responding to each of her thoughts. They took her back into the womb before birth and replaced all the memories of pain and hurt throughout her childhood with memories of love. During this time, she fell asleep.

When Jenny woke up at 10:00 the next morning, she was in her own bed and thought for sure she had just been in another dream. But her body did not hurt anywhere, and she felt really amazing! Besides, she no longer wanted to wonder which scenes were reality and which scenes were dreams. She knew her life would continue to appear, just as she emotionally felt it, into existence.

Jenny headed for her bathroom to brush her teeth, and there on the sink was a white eight-inch long and one-inch round device that looked just like the one she had seen on the ET ship. When she picked it up, a telepathic message came into her mind and instructed her how to use it. She touched the end of it to a spot on her forearm that had begun to throb. The device vibrated softly upon impact, and after about a minute, the sore spot was gone.

Other instructions came into Jenny's mind about using the device to heal other people. Then a flash-drive materialized before her, and she was told that it had healing sounds on it as well as subliminal rebirth instructions similar to what she experienced in the rainbow-colored pool. The sounds would change magically according to what the listener needed to hear to heal. She was to use the massage table she already had and invite people to experience healing through the sounds and the device she now had.

After the first person experienced a healing through the sound and the device, that person told others who began to come. Jenny also went to the elderly people she knew and used it on them as well. The technique was working on every kind of problem whether it was healing a broken bone or healing cancer. Her chiropractor asked her to do this new "Physical Therapy" for patients who came to his office, so she did this as well.

Financial abundance soon followed, and Jenny was thrilled to have more than enough for herself as well as having funds to donate to many of her favorite causes. She treated people no matter what their financial ability to pay was. She met other health practitioners who used massage, Reiki, reflexology, acupuncture, etc. who networked their services with her own. She coordinated meditation circles with all these practitioners to focus on peace for the planet.

The ETs were satisfied of their choice of human to give their healing technology to. Jenny knew that merely 100 people meditating on peace as if it already existed could stop the destruction the Earth had been headed for.

Other well-known world authors and teachers like Gregg Braden, Bruce Lipton, and Oprah Winfrey contacted Jenny offering to pay her travel expenses to their homes in Hawaii and other island resorts. They, too, were organizing group meditations for transforming Earth. Jenny would never again have thoughts of not having enough because she would forever have more than enough of everything for herself and all the people she loved.

Other Books by Renee Alter

Appearances:
  A Journey of Self-Discovery

Reflections:
  A Toolbox of Poetry

Love, Life, & God:
  Getting Past the Pain

View From A Tree

Creating A Meaningful Life After Disability:
  Posts From My Blog

Blog Therapy:
  Posts From My Blog Part 2

Miracles Sandwiched Between the Challenges:
  Making It Through The Roller Coasters Of My Life
  With The Help Of My Guardian Angels
  (Short Story)

Growing An Internal Garden to Cope With
  Chronic Pain, Illness, & Depression

Alternative Realities:
  Daydreams of Conversations

The Land of Mark
  (Short Story-Kindle & Audible)

The Adventures of Gnat
  (Short Story-Kindle & Audible)

Twin Flame
  (Short Story-Kindle & Audible)